More by the Author

The Reztap Chronicles

Book Zero
Mishaps and Mayhem

Book One
The Adventures of Reztap

Book Two
The Quest for the Insane Moth

The Chronicles of Reztap
Book Zero

MISHAPS AND MAYHEM

ARTEMUS WITHERS

BLUE FORGE PRESS
Port Orchard, Washington

Mishaps and Mayhem
Copyright 2015, 2022
by Artemus Withers

First eBook Edition November 2018
First Print Edition November 2018
Second Print Edition April 2022

Cover art by Jerrica Law
Interior design by Brianne DiMarco

ISBN 978-1-59092-965-0

For information about film, reprint or other subsidiary rights, contact: blueforgegroup@gmail.com

Blue Forge Press is the print division of the volunteer-run, federal 501(c)3 nonprofit company, Blue Forge Group, founded in 1989 and dedicated to bringing light to the shadows and voice to the silence. We strive to empower storytellers across all walks of life with our four divisions: Blue Forge Press, Blue Forge Films, Blue Forge Gaming, and Blue Forge Records. Find out more at www.BlueForgeGroup.org

Blue Forge Press
7419 Ebbert Drive Southeast
Port Orchard, Washington 98367
blueforgepress@gmail.com
360-550-2071 ph.txt

DEDICATION

This book is dedicated to my mother, Gail, who always kept her cool even when I was sometimes finger painting with my own poop. Happily, I've matured somewhat since then.

ACKNOWLEDGEMENTS

I want to thank Megan LaFollett, formerly of Chart House Press, for putting the idea of this book into my head. I thoroughly enjoyed working on it. The laughs I've heard out loud from readers always bring a smile to my face.

Big thank you to Blue Forge Press for taking a chance and bringing *The Chronicles of Reztap* back to life! I would have gotten the books back in print eventually, but not with a top notch crew like the one at Blue Forge Press!

THE CHRONICLES OF REZTAP
BOOK ZERO

MISHAPS
AND
MAYHEM

ARTEMUS WITHERS

Part One

A Little Misunderstanding

CHAPTER 1
A SLIGHT IMPERFECTION

All I'm asking for is fewer death-defying missions," Barnabus said as he flipped his long blonde hair back over his shoulder. Tar looked annoyed at our navigator, but I'm not sure if it was because of his long luxurious hair or his propensity for stating the obvious.

"Last year was incredibly profitable," Tar said. He then went back to calibrating the holographic projectors. He'd been pinched uncomfortably during his last session with them.

"That is true," I added, but I knew where Barnabus was going and my addition wasn't anywhere near sufficient enough to distract him from his ultimate target.

"We were profitable because of the one mission we undertook that wasn't forced on us by your psychopathic brother!"

"Half-brother," Tar said as he continued adjusting the projectors. I was amazed he didn't even break his concentration to reply, but then we'd had this argument dozens of times in the last two years, so he may have just been using muscle memory to control his mouth and vocal cords.

"I don't care about the myriad interconnected and equally dysfunctional, disconnected branches of your family tree. I just want to be at death's door less often than I cash a paycheck."

Tar closed the housing on the projector.

"Got it!" he exclaimed and handed the projector to me.

"You agree then?" Barnabus asked.

"What?" Tar replied. Using my height, I pushed the projector into place inside the imaging room. It clicked and I turned the clasps holding it in place. A green light went on signifying full connectivity, so I stopped turning the clasps.

"Have you even been listening?" Barnabus turned a bit red in the face. It was a shame since he had such a nice complexion and the red discolored it unevenly. If he knew what it did to his model worthy good looks, I was certain he'd refrain from getting upset. Upon self-reflection, I mused I might be slightly jealous of his abilities with the ladies.

"You have some amazing solution to stop us from having to encounter my half brother," Tar said as he turned around in the imaging chamber and faced me. He gave me a thumbs-up. I turned the unit on.

A woman with her dark hair in a tight bun and dressed in a maroon, leather pantsuit appeared next to him. He turned and raised his hand as if to speak. She slapped him soundly across the face before he could say anything. His shoulders slumped and he looked at me. I turned the program off and the woman disappeared.

"Yes, I believe I do," Barnabus said. Tar looked at him in confusion.

"Do what? Oh, right... continue," Tar said as he stepped out of the imaging chamber and approached me.

"I have gone through an incredibly complex series of go-betweens and contacts outside the Republic's influence to setup our next trade run," Barnabus said as he brought up a schematic on the bridge viewscreen of two dozen contacts with lines connecting them. I noticed several outside the normal sphere of the Republic's influence.

"She's not supposed to slap me," Tar said as he looked at the smaller display in front of me showing the parameters for the holographic imaging system.

"At least she didn't pinch you."

"Only because her hand was fully formed this time. She's supposed to lovingly caress my cheek."

"Maybe you have the wrong program in." I pointed at the title which read *Mistress Donna Shows You Who's Boss*. Tar frowned.

"Huh. Same actress. Wrong program."

Barnabus cleared his throat and we looked at him. I tapped Tar's arm and pointed at Barnabus' schematic.

"Well, that's a lot of trouble to avoid someone who's unavoidable," Tar said as he walked up to the schematic and looked at the names and places.

"It ends with Harquoth Ellitz, a known supplier of goods to people who have a beef with the Republic," Barnabus said as he folded his arms.

"That's code for smuggler," Tar said and walked back to me.

"It's legitimate, time sensitive cargo. We're the closest trader who can handle it in the time needed."

"How convenient," I said as I watched Tar type in *Actuary Donna Takes A Loss*. I looked at Tar.

"She's an emotional accountant..." Tar trailed off as he searched for the right words to describe this particular program. I imagined a small thermonuclear meltdown somewhere in his cerebral cortex as it gave up the hunt. "It's complicated."

"Artificially created stem cells that have a limited life span in suspended animation are needed by the experimental lab on Quanos. They took two weeks longer to finish than expected and the previously contracted trader had to go onto his next job."

"So it's not illegal cargo?" Tar asked as he stepped back into the imaging chamber and I started the program. Actuary Donna appeared, this time with luxurious dark curls flowing down over her flower dress. She gently caressed Tar's cheek with her right hand and then lowered it as she slapped him with the left hand. He looked at me and smiled. I shook my head.

"It's perfectly legal in all the sectors of space we'll be traversing."

"So we're in the right place at the right time," Tar said.

"Exactly," Barnabus said smiling.

"Well, I don't see any reason not to go for it then. Lay in a course and let's get after it!" Tar said.

"Done. Signaling acceptance of the contract now. We should be there in two days."

"You know this is a trap," I whispered to Tar.

"Undoubtedly, but if it makes Barnabus happy..." Tar said and shrugged his shoulders.

"You got the helm, Barnabus?" I asked.

Barnabus gave me a thumbs-up.

"We'll be back in a few then," I said and grabbed

Tar's arm. Since I was a tall, muscular man and Tar was more, shall we say, diminutive, he could do little to protest me dragging him from the bridge. We got into the turbo lift and when the doors shut, I cocked my head inquisitively. He raised his eyebrows. I raised mine back. He crossed his arms. I frowned.

"What?" Tar asked.

"Make Barnabus happy?" I crossed my arms and narrowed my eyes. "Since when do you ever want to make Barnabus happy? You're usually at each other's throat."

"Well, navigators are hard to come by nowadays," Tar said, and turned toward the door like that was the end of the conversation. We'd been together too long. I knew when he was hiding something which he only did if it was particularly bad news.

"They're not that hard to come by, even if we can't get credentialed ones anymore. Spill it."

The turbo lift door opened and Tar stepped out. "Care for a cool beverage to quench your parched throat?"

I followed Tar to our plain, utilitarian galley. The design scheme was metal on metal with a side helping of metal. I sat down on a bar stool. Tar popped open a bottle of sparkling water and handed it to me.

"Shouldn't there be something stronger to drink for this conversation?" I asked, knowing we were low on intoxicating beverages. Tar grimaced.

"After that close call last mission with the meat grinder," Tar said.

"I never told him how close he came to being *Barnabus* brand sausage links," I noted before taking a swig. The bubbles tickled, but there was no intoxicating effect.

"Well, I made some inquiries. You know, just in

case we needed to replace our navigator."

"Again."

"Exactly." Tar sat on one of the jump seats attached to the galley wall. It was one of the only things in the galley that didn't look metallic, but it was not what you'd call a design choice. It was more of an afterthought. "We have something of a reputation."

I closed my eyes. Visions of our previous navigator Mordu whisked off planet by bounty hunters never ceased to grow my appetite for alcohol.

"Mordu's apprehension wasn't our fault," I said.

"Well, in all fairness, we did advise him not to get the plastic surgery," Tar replied.

I rubbed my bald head and sighed.

"He needed a new nose. It wasn't going to grow back on its own."

"If he hadn't angered the Kattakas, he wouldn't have suffered any facial injuries." Tar took a swig of his drink and sighed.

"Technically, he was still alive when he left our employ."

"Wish that was true of the others, then we wouldn't have the reputation of being cursed."

I stood up and tossed my empty bottle into the recycling chute.

"Really? Superstition in today's society?"

Tar shrugged. "We have a bad track record. News spreads quicker than Yangolian jelly."

"So you think walking into a trap will improve our record?"

"I didn't say it was a perfect plan."

CHAPTER 2
PARADE OF FOOLS

It wasn't that I didn't trust Barnabus, but I knew he gave people too much credit. That was a bonus for us; otherwise, we might not be running around with a flesh and blood navigator. The down side was trusting people like Harquoth to be what they said they were–legit.

I ran the checks myself and came up with the same result as Barnabus. Harquoth was squeaky clean. To me this just meant he was dirty and incredibly successful. No one had a clean record. It took a lot of money to get everything expunged and the only reason to do it was to run a high level smuggling operation with little fear of successful prosecution.

Harquoth had a trading license with the Republic. According to the records, he paid the necessary tariffs and fees and was in good standing with the authorities. The cleaner his record looked, the dirtier it must be in reality. Unfortunately, the cleaners were so good, I couldn't find a trace of a clue about what

Harquoth was really into or what we might be getting ourselves into.

Two solid days of meticulous digging and I had unearthed bupkis.

Eleera was a small moon of a gas giant in the RS-201-221-451 system. They didn't bother naming the gas giant, but I heard the local workers referred to it as His Royal Fartness. Eleera was not a gathering place for intellectual types.

The remoteness of the system was part of the attraction to putting a colony out here away from prying eyes and pesky safety regulations designed to keep everyone on the moon alive. Regulations were such a hassle. If there wasn't a major galactic conglomerate behind the colony's founding and operation, it would be a true frontier establishment. Luckily, the suits wanted some order and discipline for their investment, no matter how outside of prying eyes they wanted the colony to be. The orbiting space station doubled as the local sheriff's office and safe haven for traders wishing to dock and do business.

We docked, and that's where the real strangeness began. The politeness of the station personnel over the communication lines had been unexpected, but not any sign of trouble. It was when we walked through the airlock and were greeted by what appeared to be all available personnel, lining the corridors smiling and nodding, that I got a true appreciation for the level of fecal matter we'd stepped into. Harquoth had rolled out the red carpet as much as one could on a remote space station and there was no justifiable reason for it.

"Isn't this awesome? We're heroes!" Barnabus said as we passed the rank and defiled of the station.

"We're dead," I whispered to Tar.

"Oh yeah," Tar replied as the color drained from his face.

"Barnabus, remember our golden rule?" I asked. Barnabus frowned and scratched his head.

"Whoever smelt it-"

"No, the other golden rule."

"Oh, if she's pretty, tip her double," Barnabus said as we passed an attractive ship's mechanic. She flashed Barnabus a smile and he smiled back.

"No!" Tar said. "The golden rule that keeps us alive."

"Sure," Barnabus said as he strutted at the head of our small processional. "If it's too good to be true, duck and cover."

"Exactly," Tar and I replied.

"But that's only if you guys arrange it!" Barnabus twirled as he walked. I must confess, I hadn't known he was that graceful, especially on an iron grate catwalk.

"Barnabus," Tar began. Barnabus stepped up into Tar's personal space. He poked his finger in Tar's chest.

"This is my score, so suck it!"

Barnabus turned back around and continued strutting down the corridor, although I noted it was less emphatic than before.

"At least he remembered the rule," I said. Tar shook his head.

"It takes painful repetition to really bring it home," Tar replied and shrugged his shoulders. He quickened his pace to catch up with Barnabus.

I glanced behind us and saw two armed guards following us. They quickly turned their attention to a besotted cargo chief who could barely stand. They glanced back in our direction between shouts at the barely vertical man.

I sighed and hurried to catch up with the others.

We walked into a faux-wood-paneled conference room adorned with ornate print replicas, implying a status which was definitely out of the reach of an honestly run establishment. It was meant to impress commoners. All it did for me was confirm my suspicions.

Harquoth Ellitz, master of the manor, sat at the far end of a metal, faux-gold-embossed conference table. His throne of red-speckled gornus hide was the only thing of real value in the room. The rest of the furnishings were as valueless as the man sitting on the throne, with the possible exception of the three chairs with pointed backs on the right side of the conference table, which appeared to be silver—or at least silver-plated—and waited like dragon's teeth for their next prey. Harquoth, a water-breathing humanoid with blue skin colored by inky black splotches, waved at the chairs and nodded, an elegant implication that we were the guests of dishonor at the meeting. I glanced at the door we came though, the only visible entrance or exit for the room, and saw the two armed guards enter and shut the door with a loud clang. They smiled pleasantly displaying several metallic capped teeth, no doubt trophies from their service to Harquoth.

"Mister Ellitz!" Barnabus shouted as he walked to his seat. "Thank you so much for this opportunity."

Tar and I hesitated to take our seats until we felt laser pistol barrels insistently nudging us between the shoulder blades. We took our seats.

No," Harquoth burbled. I noticed what appeared to be a thin layer of water all around his body and realized he was likely inside a suit or force field of some kind providing a constant liquid environment for his skin and respiratory system. "It is I who must thank you for coming to me in my hour of need."

Barnabus sat comfortably back in the chair, oblivious to the armed guards who flanked me and Tar.

"Lovely chairs, Mister Ellitz," I said. The smooth metallic surface was made of an aluminum alloy of some sort. I mused it may be to resist magnetization or electrical conductivity, but for the life of me I couldn't discern why. Tar was equally curious and actually poked and prodded the arms of the chair. I glanced down to see evidence of a pit that might open and drop us into a bubbling cauldron or something of that sort, but the floor looked solid.

"Aren't they, though? A gift from a good friend." Harquoth smiled, revealing a row of small, razor-sharp teeth. "Please, call me Harky. All my close friends do."

"Before you eat them?" Tar murmured. Barnabus glared at Tar.

Harquoth laughed a wet, sloshing chuckle that sounded like children drowning.

"I heard you were entertaining, Tar," Harquoth said, sounding genuinely amused. This only heightened my level of concern. I glanced at the door and a laser pistol barrel pressed against my cheek returned my attention to our host.

"I'm sorry if Tar offended you, Harky," Barnabus said. "We just wanted to pick up the stem cell shipment and get it delivered as soon as possible."

"No," Harquoth said as manacles burst from under the armrests and legs of our three chairs, securing our wrists and ankles. "It is I who must apologize for the little white lie my benefactor helped me come up with to get you here. There is no stem cell cargo. The only shipment will actually be you, serving as payment for my trading... mmm... anomaly. Captain Bartlett agreed to forgive my accidental embargo mix-up if I delivered you to him mostly unharmed."

Barnabus' jaw hung open. He blinked rapidly as his carefully laid plan disintegrated before his eyes like Tar's morals at a brothel.

"Renni," Tar whispered.

"Ah, yes. Your dear brother supplied these chairs. They've been deemed too inhumane for official Republic business. I got a little government surplus for my troubles."

"Half brother," Tar said as he pulled on the manacles.

"You guys suck," Barnabus said as he glared at us.

"He requested I use them to get you all ready for delivery to his approaching flagship. I must confess," Harquoth said as he placed his webbed fingers in a contemplative arch and clicked his claws together rhythmically. "I'm curious what 'inhumane' means for an air breather."

The manacles began to buzz, vibrate, and glow with a blue light. A few seconds later, a searing pain permeated my body. I barely discerned the screams of the others above my own.

Everything went mercifully dark.

Chapter 3
A High Brow Moment

I hadn't expected the brow ridges when I awoke—shackles or a cell, yes—but subdermal implants in my forehead were totally unexpected.

Touching the new additions to my face, I sat up on the medical gurney and looked around. Tar watched me glumly from his own bed.

"He's not going to be happy when he wakes up," Tar said.

"Well, I'm not happy either," I said. My mouth was dry, probably from the anesthetic they used to keep us under while they modified our appearance. I spotted a clear pitcher full of liquid and a few cups on a small table by the wall. It was probably water, but I was hopeful for grain alcohol.

"I'm overjoyed!" Tar said as he pointed to his forehead. The six protrusions jutting from his brow caused a unique, jagged shadow on his face. "Had it just been four bumps, I would've been merely thrilled."

I picked up the pitcher and poured the liquid in a cup. As I poured I studied the curious change in skin coloration around my wrists. It faded from a dark color around the hands into my own natural dark shade. When I finished pouring, I took at sip of what sadly proved to be water. I finished the cup and poured some more. I glanced at Tar's hands and noticed the same type of colorization, just a lighter shade given his lighter complexion.

Barnabus stirred. He opened his eyes and I saw his facial muscles attempt to contort into a frown. His skin was stretched so tight over the horny protrusions in his brow that he was unable to frown. His hands rose to his face. Slowly he sat up and glared at Tar.

Tar sat up and shrugged at him.

"This is your score, not mine."

Barnabus opened his mouth to reply, but a smug baritone voice cut him off, issued from the speakers overhead.

"Ah, the brave adventurers awaken from their peaceful slumber."

We all looked up and noticed an observation window fifteen feet above the room. The unmistakable, bloated visage of Tar's thrice-cursed half brother, Rennifej Bartlett, stared down at us in puffy glee. I thought I noticed a trace of gray on his slimy slack temples, but that may have just been a reflection of the light. I wasn't in favor of anything that might make him look distinguished.

"Never a pleasure," I replied. I looked at Tar but my attention was immediately drawn to Barnabus who mouthed multiple disturbing curse words silently while waving his arms madly. Tar scratched his head as he looked at Barnabus.

"I took the liberty of temporarily paralyzing your

verbose navigator's vocal cords. Based on our last meeting, I found his vulgar ranting tiresome."

Barnabus made several gestures and movements that made it perfectly clear he didn't need his voice to communicate vulgarity. Once he finished, he sat on the bed and fumed.

"Such a pleasant girly man," Renni said and sniffed. Barnabus made an obscene finger gesture.

"You done posturing, thug nut?" Tar asked.

"Ah, baby brother finds his ever-respectful tongue at last!" Renni exclaimed.

"Half bro- AHHH!" Tar screamed the last part and sank to his knees, holding his head.

"I took the additional liberty of adding remote control electrodes to your subdermal implants, Tar. I'm glad to see the extra precautions weren't in vain."

"Are you trying to kill me, psycho?"

"So dramatic," Renni said. He paused for a moment to belch and take a whiff. "Exquisite lunch. The electrodes are calibrated to cause extreme pain but no permanent damage."

"You should have them implanted in your crotch," Tar said just before the anticipated jolt of pain laid him out on the floor.

"Perhaps the past should stay in the past, Reztap."

"Perhaps." Tar groaned in between gasps for breath.

"I assume, Captain Bartlett, that the subdermal implants we received aren't just to improve our luck with the ladies," I said, hoping to bring the antagonistic display of sibling rivalry to an end.

"Gorth, always the pragmatist," Renni said. He sighed, perhaps reluctant to end Tar's pain so soon. "A simple delivery to the Claché embassy on Progor Three to facilitate an expeditious, peaceful end to the negotiations between the Progorians and Clachés. Unfortunately, Republic forces have been forbidden from direct involvement in the negotiations."

"Been told to stay out of the pool again?" Tar said and quickly continued before Renni could activate his pain protocol. "You want us to be war spies? What would mother say?"

"Tools of peace."

"How do you get credit for this then?" I asked. I then swallowed nervously. I hadn't meant to speak it out loud as it might offend the intensely ambitious captain who preferred to work anonymously behind the scenes to further his career.

"Peace between these people will stabilize the region, improving trade relations, opening valuable trade routes..."

"Making the sector you patrol more valuable to the Republic, thereby increasing its importance and your status," I said, completing his thought.

Renni smiled. It wasn't pleasant to see. I repressed the urge to vomit. Barnabus failed and hurled a rainbow of colors onto the floor. I believe Tar had built up an immunity.

"The best part, of course, is that should you fail, all I've lost is a pesky half-breed relative and his scurrilous crew."

Barnabus stepped lightly around his vomit and mooned Renni.

"Enough of this foolishness!" Renni said. "Your Claché embassy shuttle is moored and awaiting you. I expect your departure within the hour after which I will continue pressing the remote on Reztap's implants until the nuclear batteries run down or you escape the 20,000-mile range of the receiver, whichever comes first."

"Renni!" Tar shouted.

"Please, take your time," Renni said and turned his back on us. An audible click let us know communication had ceased.

"A natural death is not soon enough for him," Tar said. "Let's get this over with."

Tar walked out of the room and I followed. We made it a few steps into the corridor before I tapped him on the shoulder. He stopped and turned around. I pointed back to the room where Barnabus had yet to emerge.

"Girly man," I said.

"Fantastic," Tar muttered and walked back into the room. I accompanied Tar and saw Barnabus, arms folded and staring at the floor.

"Barnabus, let's go," Tar said.

Barnabus glanced at him and then stared at the floor again.

"You wanted to outsmart a captain of the Republic. It didn't work, but nice try."

I walked back to my gurney and sat down.

"It's not my fault, Barnabus. It's his... and yours," I said and laid down on the gurney. I figured a nap would do me good before I had to carry Tar's electrode-tortured body back to the embassy shuttle.

"You're not helping, you know," Tar said as he looked at me.

"I'm ever the pragmatist."

Tar shook his head and turned back to Barnabus.

"If we wait much longer, I'm going to be in a tremendous amount of pain."

Barnabus looked at Tar, smiled and nodded.

"Or we could just leave you here."

After pursing his lips for a few seconds, Barnabus slumped his shoulders and waved at the door.

Tar walked out and Barnabus followed. I was half hoping Barnabus would call Tar's bluff and we could've left Long Hair there.

CHAPTER 4
A PLEASANT ENCOUNTER WITH THE ANGEL OF DEATH

The Claché embassy shuttle was one sumptuous ride. I never gave riding in the lap of luxury much thought before, but the accoutrements on this top-of-the-line vessel made me seriously reconsider it.

My parents had been treated to royal welcomes in the past. In my youth, I hadn't fully appreciated the insane creature comforts we enjoyed. I recalled the rare materials, shiny embellishments, amazing views, and food that often escaped description but was so good it was a life changing experience. Even so, either my memory was clouded by my youth, a lot had changed in luxury accommodations in the preceding fifteen years or we'd been shorted the full luxury catalog.

The command bridge sported a liquid metal surface that looked so real I thought I would sink into it upon entry. It looked like it was infused with blue sapphire crystals powered by cold fusion. A cold and powerful beast ready to be unleashed at any moment; that was just the floors and walls. As I took my seat, the liquid metal surface conformed and adjusted perfectly to my body. I'd never felt a more comfortable and relaxing seat in my life.

As I rumbled with pleasure, the seat took on a subtle royal purple hue. The seat or the ship had somehow tapped into my subconscious and found my favorite color. I felt calm, relaxed and totally focused. There was likely some sort of chemical enhancement occurring either airborne or through the skin, but I couldn't discern the source or even an odor.

The air lit up with semi-transparent screens seeming to float in midair. At a touch, the star systems on a screen in front of Barnabus leaped into the air in a dazzling holographic display. The orientation of the solar systems centered on him as a small dotted line appeared, weaving its way throughout the suspended cosmos revealing our trajectory. The highlighted path curved and turned, taking advantage of every gravity node along the way to increase our speed and efficiency.

I thought about the weaponry on the ship and was immediately treated to an in-depth schematic of the weapons and targeting systems. They were accompanied by a blinking advisory to only use them for defense as this was a diplomatic vessel. With such a reactive and advanced vehicle, we could go anywhere and do anything with nary a problem.

I glanced over to see what Tar might have pulled up using the advanced systems on the ship. There was nothing in front of him. It was about that time I heard his distinct snoring timbre reverberating through the bridge. He definitely felt relaxed and focused.

"Barnabus, you ready to get us there so we can get sleeping beauty into something less pleasant?"

Barnabus gave me a thumbs-up and there was a change in the blue hue of the ship surfaces to a more reddish hue. It was still subtle, but perceptible enough to know there had been a change. I didn't feel any physical momentum, so the flawless anti-gravity systems on board did an amazing job of countering every change in trajectory from maneuvering thrusters.

"This must be what it's like to float on a cloud," I said.

Barnabus gave me another thumbs-up and then waved. I soon heard another snore, but more of a whistling rasp then Tar's snore.

Minutes upon the most advanced vessel we'd ever been on and all they could think of was sleep.

"That's really one of the best ways to face transition. Are you ready to sleep?" a female voice asked. Her voice was so light and ethereal, I could've sworn I was communing with an angel.

"Well, that sounds really... transition?"

"Many prefer to be asleep when they experience transition."

I suddenly felt a little less calm.

"I'm sorry," I said as I watched our plotted trajectory on the suspended holographic map moving further towards our destination. "What exactly is transition?"

"Transition is the change of physical being from one plane of existence to the next," the eerily angelic voice told me as if she was explaining how to clean a window.

"You mean death?"

"Well, that's not very poetic," the voice complained.

"Um, why are we transitioning?"

"Oh, that's very simple. The Progorians typically require a live sacrifice in order for their battleships to not wipe out a small city, outpost or military installation. It's really very efficient and cuts down dramatically on casualties."

"But we're not a sacrifice," I said, hoping the angelic voice had some kind of logic circuitry in its subroutines of death and relaxation.

"Oh, yes, sometimes the sacrificial ones try that tactic. Are you sure you wouldn't like to sleep through your transition?"

"Tar! Barnabus! Wake up!" I shouted as I stood up from what I still had to admit was a really awesome seat. I just didn't relish it being my last.

"Oh dear, I'm afraid I can't let you wake them up. I don't think they would want to be awake through transition," she said and the ship's metallic surface switched back to a subtle blue. "Did the color scheme indicating the ship's movement upset you? I've changed it back to the tranquil blue of a hydrogen atom for you."

"That's really not helping. Why do you think we're destined for transition?"

"Well," the voice responded and changed the subtle blue to a kind of yellow sunflower hue. "On the way to our final transition, the ship was intercepted and the occupants removed. I chatted with a nice large man about our ship's purpose. He was very delighted by our plan."

"I'm sure Captain Bartlett was very excited," I said and rubbed my new forehead implants in frustration.

"Someone did call him Captain, now that you

mention it."

I looked around the cabin for access panels or controls, but all I saw was liquid metal.

"But he did say you were the new sacrifices and changed the destination."

"For the last time, we're not sacrifices!"

"Oh," she said. I breathed a sigh of relief until all the surfaces of the ship turned into panels, buttons and switches. "Would you like to play with instrument panels during transition? I have many different models on file."

"No, no, no! Ugh! I just need to sit down and think."

A seat formed beneath me and I sat down. It turned the loveliest shade of royal purple and then I was asleep.

CHAPTER 5
OUT OF THE FRYING PAN, INTO THE CHURCH

Alarm klaxons broke my sweet reverie on the coast of New Orleans, sipping Hurricanes with my sisters as we listened to a smooth jazz band playing "Sweet Caroline." The glaring red glowing liquid metal bridge worried me at first. I realized we should be dead and was marginally less worried, but the alarms were still quite troubling. Tar and Barnabus stood up and I followed suit.

"What's happening?" Tar shouted above the blaring alarm.

"Not sure. We should be dead, but we're not, so I'll count this as a good thing," I shouted back.

"What?" Barnabus asked. He then felt his throat and again said "What?" He threw his arms up in celebration. "I have my voice back!"

"Probably not a good thing," I shouted to Tar.

Tar looked at the surfaces of the bridge and didn't

see any controls. He moved his hands about and looked for things to appear in mid-air. Nothing happened. He sat back down in the chair and it didn't conform to his body. Luckily, it supported him and didn't drop him on the floor.

"Maybe the AI is busted," I shouted. The alarms stopped.

"I'm not busted," the computer said. "We have a faulty destination. I'm afraid I won't be able to bring you to final transition after all."

"What a shame," I said.

"Final transition?" Tar asked.

"This ship is a ritual sacrifice of three Claché lives to appease a Progorian battleship to avoid Armageddon level bloodshed."

Barnabus sat down and put his head in his hands. "You guys are Armageddon."

"Hey, we're not dead. Ship, can we go to Progor Three now?" Tar asked.

"My name is Alix," the ship responded. The liquid metal surfaces briefly flashed a brighter red.

"Alix," I said. "Can we go to Progor Three now, please?"

"Of course, we're going to Progor Three. It says specifically in the order for transition the ship must return to its point of origin, Progor Three, if it's unable to complete its mission."

We all sat down and breathed a sigh of relief.

"Awesome," Tar said. He waved his hands in front of him and a display of a star chart came up.

"But wait," Alix said. "This is a faulty transition order, so I can't obey that directive."

We all sat up in our chairs.

"And that means?" Tar asked.

"We return to our launching facility on Progor

Two, of course."

"No, no. Progor Two is not right," Tar said. "We need to be on Progor Three!"

"Well, well, aren't we a testy little sacrifice. Don't worry, in all likelihood, you will still get to experience a glorious, fireball of a transition when we get to Progor Two as most ships returning with an unfiled flight plan are shot down. Your death will not have been in vain."

I watch the dotted line taking us toward Progor Two. At our rate of speed, we'd enter the atmosphere in less than two minutes. It would probably be anywhere from thirty seconds to a few more minutes before an intercepting missile obliterated us from the sky once and for all.

"Alix, are there escape pods on the ship?"

"Of course there are, Gorth. The highest safety protocols are followed to ensure that in the event of an accidental launch, sacrificial handlers are not trapped on board a flight to their own unscheduled transition."

I stood up and paced the liquid floors of the bridge. Each step glowed as my foot came down. It was really quite spectacular to see.

"If our transition has failed, we cannot fulfill our original transition contract if we're transitioned during a re-entry to Progor Two."

There were a few moments of silence as Alix mulled over my logic.

"I have to return to Progor Two, that's my programming."

"But do you need us to return with you? We'd really like to be able to fulfill our transition contract even if we're not able to do it on board this ship."

Tar looked at me and tried to raise his eyebrows. He failed and looked up at the protruding ridges over his eyes.

"It does make sense for you to transition in the appropriate location, I suppose," Alix said. A door opened up and a single escape pod with four seats in it became visible.

"Thank you, Alix," I said. I grabbed Barnabus as we walked to the pod. He resisted.

"We're just trading one death for another, you know. I mean, eventually, anywhere you guys go, there's an inevitable death sentence on you and anyone around you."

"Let's debate it aboard the escape pod," I said.

"Are you sure you don't want to stay?" Alix asked. "I'm packed with some pretty impressive munitions to create a really spectacular fireball, visible from three hundred thousand miles away with the naked eye."

I did some mental calculations in my head and realized even in an escape pod, we may not get far enough away from the impending explosion to escape harm.

"Wow," I said.

"One death for another," Barnabus said.

"Get in!" Tar shouted. We ran to the escape pod.

"Have a great transition, Alix!" I shouted as we strapped into our seats.

"You too!" she replied.

The pod doors shut and it ejected from the bosom of the mother ship. We felt the effects of gravity and centrifugal force as the pod began spinning. While I normally would've been glad to have a window to see what was going on outside, this time I was happy to be visually ignorant.

Thirty seconds later, the pressure wave from what must have been Alix's glorious transition hit the escape pod, spinning us in the opposite direction and then end over end. Perhaps another minute into our free fall, there was a small explosion and the escape pod jerked us around in our seats as a rescue parachute caught us in the atmosphere and slowed our descent.

"Hey, at least we're not dead," Tar said.

An alarm sounded.

"I really wish you'd stop saying that," Barnabus said.

Lights flashed and an overhead speaker blared out "Parachute integrity at eighty percent."

"See that's not so bad," Tar said and smiled. Even I felt an urge to punch him.

"Parachute integrity at seventy percent."

"You guys really need an edge. Might I suggest praying to a deity or something when you're at the lip of a volcano about to erupt?" Barnabus said.

"We don't really have deities on Andros."

"We have plenty on Terra," I said. "An overabundance, really."

"Parachute integrity at sixty percent."

The pod vibrated from the increasing turbulence.

"What about where you're from, Barnabus?" Tar asked.

"We really take more of a neo-classic natural approach to the order of things. I don't necessarily recommend a utilitarian approach to the cosmos like I believe in. I really think you guys need help from some kind of spooky entity to pull your fat out of the fire."

"Parachute integrity at fifty-percent," the voice droned on as the turbulence increased.

"We'll take that into consideration," I said.

"You realize I still think you guys suck."

"Yeah," Tar said.

"Parachute integrity at thirty-percent."

There was a loud crack and the turbulence stopped. We looked at each other nervously.

"Parachute failed. Prepare for crash landing."

"How about just a generic 'God'?" Tar said.

"That's works for me. Covers most of the ones on my planet and is a sure plug-in for many other worlds," I said.

"Umm, OK. Uh, hop in any time now, God!"

"Hmm, not sure that's how it's done. We'll look it up," I said and grabbed the straps of my safety harness. A red light illuminated us.

"Please hold your breath for twenty seconds as we prepare your bodies for impact," the pleasant voice said as if we were simply pulling on a jumpsuit and getting ready for the day. We all held our breath and a quick-acting impact foam immediately burst forth from the nozzles around our seats, covering us in a cocoon of impact resistance. The foam hardened within a second or two of hitting our bodies.

We felt a few shakes and then the foam dissipated. We sat in darkness, unaware of where we had landed on Progor Two.

Chapter 6
Public Enemy Number One-ish

Aren't there supposed to be emergency lights or something?" Barnabus inquired.

"How many crash landings have you been in?" I asked.

"We had some simulations in navigator survival school. How many have you been in?"

"More than this one," Tar said quickly. I took it the actual number was higher than Tar was comfortable with Barnabus hearing. I didn't think it would matter much. Barnabus staying on as navigator seemed an increasingly remote possibility with each passing minute.

A single red light burst to life. I confirmed with my eyes what my inner ear told me. The door to the escape pod was at a thirty-degree angle upward from our seats. With the grated floor and ceiling, we could have traversed the interior of the pod had it landed at pretty much any angle and reached the door. None of us knew what was on the other side of the sealed hatch.

"Well," I said as I popped the connections open on my harness. "Let's see what we've gotten ourselves into."

"See Tar, that's a lot better than saying 'at least we're not dead.'"

I twisted the wheel on the hatch and then pushed it open with a clang. I stuck my head out and saw a lot of rubble below me. Out beyond the rubble, a long line of trucks, cameras and military personnel were lining up to take aim on the pod. Up above me, a dozen flying vehicles hovered, some with cameras and others with various types of weaponry pointed at us. I dropped back down.

"Hmm, I kind of wish we'd died," I said.

Barnabus put his face in his hands. The bumps forced him to move his palms down to his cheeks and stare forward.

"Is it bad?" Tar asked.

"Let's just say we didn't manage to sneak in and out quietly."

Within minutes, the pod was swarming with four-foot tall lizard-like Progorians aiming weapons and shouting orders. We had no choice but to surrender quietly as they strapped us into harnesses and raised us up to one of the hovering ships. As I went up into the air, I looked down and saw a mob forming around the crash site. I heard the angry shouts as they waved sticks and other improvised weapons at our party. The building below looked to be made of some kind brick, but it was damaged beyond all recognition. I didn't know what the pod had landed on or if anyone had been killed.

It took roughly twenty minutes to get to the base where these soldiers had come from. We landed and were marched inside at gun point. I had to duck down to go through the doorways as the Progorians were much shorter than average humanoids and built their buildings to their specifications. The room we were left in had a large screen on one wall and short chairs, again designed for much smaller humanoids. We all sat uncomfortably on the chairs for a few minutes before a Progorian smoking a cigar and wearing a suit came in smiling.

"How you guys doing?" the Progorian said as he pulled up a chair and sat on it backwards in front of us.

"We're doing okay. Look we're sorry about the mess," Tar said.

"Ah, don't worry about it. The press has done a great job with it. Check this out," the Progorian said and turned on the screen behind him.

A lizard woman with dark flowing hair looked towards us on the screen with a microphone in her hand.

"The bloodthirsty invaders swiftly pounced upon the congregation of this poor unsuspecting church, full of worshipers for the evening service," she said as the camera panned behind her and showed our escape pod which had crushed a building just a little bit larger than the pod. Just from a quick estimation, I figured there couldn't have been more than ten people in the small building.

"Hundreds of people were crushed in this horrible attack, leaving the town reeling with anguish and anger."

"Hundreds?" I said. The Progorian smiled at me

and waved.

"Oh wait," he said. "It gets better."

The camera showed the reporter with her microphone in front of another woman, this one with reddish hair.

"It was horrible! They came out, swinging long blades and just cutting the heads off children!"

"And priests?" the reporter asked.

"That's right and priests! They even slaughtered the children's puppies!"

"Uh," Tar said. "What's going on?"

"Hold on," the Progorian said and turned up the volume as a Progorian couple hugged each other and cried. The reporter came up to them with the microphone.

"Our babies were in there! What will we ever do?" they cried and the camera turned back to the reporter.

"There you have it. A terrible tragedy in Lasitown as Claché barbarians attack a poor innocent parish, slaughtering everyone inside. A unified voice has called out from the community for the summary execution of the beasts from above. Ana Seezore, Flywitness News."

The Progorian turned off the TV as it went to the next story.

"That Ana is delicious, I'd love to break insects with her. Crack news team. Damn near put me in tears with their efficiency and hard work. Makes my job so much easier."

I'm not sure which one of us stopped staring at the screen with our jaw hung open first. Barnabus was the first one to speak.

"That's not what happened."

The Progorian got up and laughed. He walked around the room laughing and then stopped, put one hand on the chair and waved at the screen.

"Don't worry about it! It's nothing. The building was empty."

I sighed with relief. The others looked visibly relieved as well.

"I am Vigrizz Penthau, but you can call me Vig. What's your name?" Vig said to our relieved navigator. I realized we hadn't been given aliases or even credentials. I wondered if Barnabus would be sharp enough to make up a believable name on the spot.

"Barnabus. Barnabus Angstead."

I closed my eyes and shook my head.

"Barnabus! That's a great name. Very thuggish, kind of like a barbarian—Barnabus. I love it."

He looked at me and raised his darkened eyebrow ridges. I looked him in his yellow eyes and watched the protective eyelid cross his eyes before he blinked.

"Frank. Frank Jones," I said.

The Progorian burst out laughing and went around the room shaking his head, having a great time—with what, I didn't know. Finally he sat back down and smiled at me.

"I figured it'd be you," he said, nodding his head and smiling. "Giving me an alias. You're smart, Gorth. Crafty. But Gorth, that name! It's so guttural. You have to go with a natural like that. The public will eat it up!"

"Eat it up?" Tar said.

The Progorian looked at Tar with a serious frown.

"Tar. Tar Reztap. This one's been bugging me, but I'm up for a challenge."

"Challenge?" Tar said and looked at me. I shrugged my shoulders. I didn't know what was going on, but I was pretty sure it wasn't good.

"Well, it's not very intimidating, is it? Tar Reztap. Nope, it doesn't scare me at all."

"Why am I supposed to be scary? Wait, I'm intimidating!" Tar said and stood up. The Progorian looked at Tar for a moment and then a big grin broke out on his face.

"Slimy. Slimy, villainous Tar Reztap! The brains behind the massacre. Oh yeah, I can sell that all day!" The Progorian rubbed his hands together and nodded his head.

"What are you talking about?" Tar threw his hands up and touched the ceiling. Vig pointed at Tar and nodded.

"Right, sorry. The subdermal implants were so good, I temporarily forgot you weren't Claché, so you wouldn't know. I really apologize. Should've brought you guys up to speed. My full title is Executional Administrator of the Third Circuit military court. I'm just your official assistant in all matters surrounding your executions."

CHAPTER 7
A CIVIL MATTER

Executions?" Barnabus said. "But we haven't done anything!"

"You killed hundreds of people in a church! Of course, we're going to execute you with prejudice." Vig stomped his burned-out cigar and lit another.

"You just said we didn't kill anyone," Tar said. He sat down. I sighed. I knew where this was going.

"Unofficially, you knocked down an abandoned building that was marked for demolition. The city of Lasitown thanks you for that. Saved us a couple dargons, really. Darn near a public service."

"Unofficially," I said.

"Right!" Vig got back up and paced the room in front of us. "The official version has a lot more punch to it. Claché mercenaries kill hundreds and demolish a church in bloodthirsty terrorist attack! Ceasefire canceled! The war is on again!"

"Whoa, whoa, whoa!" Tar said getting up. "We were just delivering a package to make the peace, not break it.”

“Package? What package?”

Tar pointed at Vig and tried to speak. He dropped his hand and tried to speak again.

Vig sat down and took a puff on his cigar.

Tar pointed at the ceiling. He put his hand down. He sat in his chair.

“It was on the shuttle.”

Vig looked down at the floor and nodded. He hemmed and hawed for a few seconds. He looked at Tar.

“Well, that's shame.” Vig got up and walked around pacing again. “Love that Alix program, though. Yeah? I would've done it a bit differently. Maybe made the sacrifices a little more scared about their coming transition, but I wasn't in charge. Claché specifications—so boring. Can you imagine being threatened with torture, maiming, being boiled alive and then the subsequent relief of knowing you're just going to be snuffed out by the thousand-degree fire of a bright star while you sleep? I really love the balance of it all. Still, Alix is a nice piece of work.”

“Can't you work with us a little bit here?” Barnabus asked.

“Oh, I am! You guys don't know how lucky you are. I am the premier executional administrator on all of Progor Two. You literally landed in the best possible place on the planet. Crazy lucky, really.”

“Uh,” Barnabus mumbled.

“Enough about me, huh? I've got some first class cells for you guys. So let's get to it!”

They were nice as cells go. Each cell had multiple beds which was convenient since we all had to combine two beds to make one large enough. I checked the bars on the windows, and they seemed pretty sturdy. I didn't see escape through the window in the dark of night happening. I looked at Tar's cell. He pulled on his window bars.

"Not going anywhere soon, are we?" Barnabus asked from his own cell.

"I'm half tempted to smash my subdermal implants against these bars to see which is tougher," Tar said.

"You might zap yourself," I said as I sat on my bed. I thought about what I said for a moment and looked up at Tar. He nodded slowly at me.

"Barnabus!" Vig shouted as he entered the cell complex. "You've been pardoned! Isn't that great?"

Barnabus stood up and walked to the cell door.

"What? That's wonderful news!" He smiled and then attempted to frown, a near impossibility with the implants. "What about Tar and Gorth?"

"Oh, yes. Well, their cases are still under review by the tribunal, but you have been cleared of all charges and I suggest we get you on the next transport out of here before the magistrate changes his mind."

Barnabus looked at us as the cell door opened. I smiled.

"Go on! We'll be on the next transport right behind you," I said. Tar gave him a thumbs-up.

"I could wait," Barnabus said as he held out his hands.

"No!" we both shouted together.

"Most important thing is for you to get to safety," Tar said. "Go to Selatarn. We'll meet you there, have a drink and laugh over the whole ordeal."

"Well, all right."

Barnabus walked out with Vig. There were no guards around them, so I assumed he was no longer under threat of death.

"So, what's the plan?" I asked.

"I split the skin open on my forehead and dig one of those electrodes out. When someone gets close enough, zap!"

"OK, sounds good, but what about-" I stopped my sentence as I watched Tar run at the bars of his cell with his forehead leading the way. There was a loud clang. Tar was flat on his back and unconscious.

"Never mind," I said. I lay down on my two Progorian cell beds and waited for the executioners to arrive or for Tar to wake up.

A few hours passed and I awoke to the sound of Vig walking back into the cell complex. I got up and stretched my arms. A good yawn got enough oxygen back in me to wake me up the rest of the way. Vig stopped at Tar's cell and looked at him. He looked back at me.

"Did he try to commit suicide? Maybe I took the wrong condemned first. I really thought Barnabus would be the first to crack," Vig said as he scratched his head with long black claws.

"Condemned?" I stood up as I talked. "I thought Barnabus was freed."

"Oh, that. Yes." Vig nodded. "A special opportunity came up and, honestly, the death by dandrin eels we had scheduled for Barnabus isn't much of a crowd pleaser. Terrible ratings usually. You know how it is though. Dandrin eel consortium bribes a few officials and then you have an unpopular execution method taking front and center stage."

Vig pointed at me. "That's what happens when you allow special interest groups to interfere with regularly scheduled programming. Damn politicians."

"Where's Barnabus now?"

"Oh yeah!" Vig brightened up and opened Tar's cell. "We had a visiting ecto beast from Tanjea on a diplomatic visit when, all of a sudden, they started gestating. Well, we didn't have any appropriate live mammals for them them to ingest to nourish their offspring during the crucial first thirty-six hours, so we improvised."

I sat down on the bed. All the energy drained out of me.

"He's dead?"

Vig looked up at the wall clock.

"Oh no, not yet. He'll be sedated, usually with a tentacle bash to induce unconsciousness. Don't want to introduce any harmful chemicals to the young in their first meal. Then he'll be fitted with a breathing mask to ensure he doesn't die immediately during the feeding process," Vig said as he examined Tar's forehead. "Then the ecto beast swallows him whole, feet first. The freshly opened birthing postules inside the ecto beast release the offspring from their protective cocoons. They latch onto Barnabus, feeding off his blood and flesh over the following twenty-four hours."

"That sounds horrible," I said. I got up and walked to the cell bars and held onto them.

"Indeed, the poor ecto beast has to spend the next twenty-four hours with a plastic breathing tube hanging out of its mouth. It can hardly talk, can't eat or drink anything else and, of course, it has to avoid slicing the breathing tube with its razor sharp teeth. Incredibly uncomfortable."

Tar reached up his hand and grabbed Vig's. A spark of electricity erupted and Vig screamed in pain and fell to the ground. Tar got up and snatched the keys from Vig's belt. Vig ignored him as he grabbed his injured hand with the other and screamed again. Tar walked out of the cell and unlocked my door.

"What next?" I asked. Tar shrugged and closed Vig's cell door. He locked it and smiled.

"Ha!" Vig said. "Where will you go? The entire planet knows what you look like. You'll be hunted down within the hour!"

"He does have a point," I said. We both looked at Vig as Tar unlocked the door.

"You came to your senses. Excellent."

"No," Tar said as he grabbed Vig's hand again. "We need you to escort us to wherever Barnabus is."

"He already left."

"Then we'll need to get a ship from there," I said. "I'll scout them out when we arrive."

"But," Vig said, "no one's ever escaped Progorian execution before!"

"Always a first time," Tar said. Vig smiled.

"That's brilliant!" Vig exclaimed. "Mass murderers execute bold escape from Progorian custody! Dozens killed as the dastardly duo blast their way off Progor Two!"

"Whatever," Tar said and walked out with Vig.

Chapter 8
Best Ratings Ever

Vig smiled as he drove through the city. I expected him to make some kind of escape attempt himself, but he seemed thoroughly content to be our prisoner. I looked out the window at the buildings whizzing by. Progorians lined the streets, shopped, ate, and generally carried on their daily lives like nothing was amiss. For a populace under the threat of impending war, they seemed fairly complacent about it.

"Gorth, with your advanced tactical weaponry knowledge and piloting expertise, you'll know the long range X-three tactical cruiser will be your best and fastest way to escape," Vig said as he slowed down to wait for cross-traffic.

"I would, huh?"

"Absolutely. I'll get you onto the command deck after I distract the skeleton crew maintaining it."

"How will you do that?" Tar asked.

"I'll tell them we lost a translation-sanity coupling

on an ecto beast and it's loose aboard their ship. They'll evacuate until the asset control team arrives to reel the ecto beast back into custody for the next show."

"Next show?"

Vig rubbed his hands together gleefully and then grabbed the wheel again as traffic cleared.

"A normal execution show draws in a few hundred million. Sure we try different methods of drawing them in, but inevitably, the death by ecto beast actually draws in billions of viewers. It's by far our most popular execution."

"Uh," I said as I looked at Tar. He grimaced and rolled his eyes. "How exactly does an ecto beast kill someone?"

"I'm so glad you asked," Vig replied.

"I'm not," Tar said and sat back trying to get as far away from the description as possible.

"The condemned is shackled hands over head, legs manacled to the floor spread eagle as the camera zooms in on his face. Of course, he's completely terrified because we've described in intimate detail how he's going to die and he knows it." Vig turned to look at me. "The more scared they are, the better the ratings. Nothing scares like an ecto beast."

"You're a bloodthirsty lot," Tar murmured.

"Oh, absolutely, primarily when it comes to our enemies. There isn't so much Progorian on Progorian violence."

"Interesting," I said. "The ecto beast?"

"Right," Vig said. He stopped at the star port entrance and flashed his credentials. The guard looked in and saw us. He scratched his head and waved us through.

"The ecto beast slowly approaches the subject,"

Vig said as he accelerated toward one of the hangars. "It shoots out a long proboscis which pierces the abdomen of the condemned and it slowly pumps digestive juices into them. The juices leave the skin and bones intact, but dissolve everything else. The condemned usually scream in excruciating pain for about thirty minutes before the digestive juices liquify the nerves and the spinal cord. It's only about ten more minutes of screen time before the digestive juices finish their path in the body. We actually take a few commercial breaks at this point since all the suffering is done. Come back from commercial, the ecto beast sucks out the entire pre-digested contents and is fully satiated for several months. Roll credits, collect ridiculous paycheck."

Tar looked green in the back seat. I hoped he wasn't going to spew digestive juices of his own.

"Why are you helping us so willingly?" Tar asked and took a deep breath. Some of the color returned to his face.

"Ratings," Vig said.

"What?"

"Don't get me wrong, we're incredibly sensitive to electricity." Vig held up his hand. There was an angry red circle where Tar had zapped him. "I don't wish to experience that again. More importantly, there has never been an escape. The ratings will go through the roof. I daresay, it will dwarf the ecto beast executions. Maybe even more important personally, that means an interview with Ana Seezore describing the Claché commando team breaking in, the ensuing battle with dozens, no, hundreds of deaths of brave Progorian soldiers and citizens trying to ensure you murderous brigands get your just rewards for your heinous crimes. That's a damn dream come true, guys."

We pulled up to the ship and two guards walked forward, guns drawn.

"You guys might want to sit further back in the seat for this," Vig said.

"I think he's on the up and up," I said to Tar. Tar nodded and we both sat back.

"These guys are a little crazy," Tar said.

"Kind of reminds me of your family get-togethers." Tar grunted.

The window rolled down and Vig waved his credentials at the two guards. One of them came to the window.

"We tracked an ecto beast onto your ship. It escaped the translation-sanity coupling—damn near tried to feed on me," Vig said as he held up his hand where Tar had caused the angry red welt on his green flesh. He also produced a small collar with multiple lights on it in his other hand. The two guards looked at one another in horror. The lead man snagged the radio from his belt.

"This is Charlie One. We have a confirmed ecto beast breach on board. All hands abandon ship! Repeat. All hands abandon ship!"

Vig pointed at a small blast proof safety bunker across the flight-line. The guards made a beeline for the building, never looking back. Seconds later, the remaining ship's personnel came streaming down the ramp of the X-three cruiser. They followed their coworkers into the bunker. Vig accelerated up the ramp and stopped in the cargo bay. He got out and opened the door for us.

"You always carry a spare ecto beast collar in your transport?" I asked.

"Are you kidding? In my business, you always have at least one spare. I've got three more under the back seat," Vig said and then turned to run up the ramp into the crew quarters. We followed him until he led us directly to the bridge and I looked around, amazed. The crew left so fast there were half eaten dinners and steaming drinks left at their stations.

"Ecto beast is heading home to Tanjea Prime. It's up to you guys now. Make me proud! I've got an interview to do," Vig said and turned his back on us and walked off the bridge. I walked over to the bridge and checked the status of the ship. Everything looked nominally functional.

"Oh, I almost forgot," Vig said as he walked back onto the bridge with a laser rifle.

"Crap," Tar said. Vig walked up to Tar and handed him the laser rifle.

"Shoot for the ecto beast's head. It can't shoot out its proboscis with your friend inside. They regenerate, so I recommend dragging the corpse to a locked cell before it becomes an uncorpse." He pointed to his scaly left cheek. "If you'd be so kind as to hit me with the rifle butt. This is my bad side."

"I might knock you out," Tar said.

Vig shook his head. "If I'd wanted to be knocked out, I would've asked Gorth to do it."

Tar growled and swung the rifle at Vig's head with all his might. Vig staggered back a few steps. He straightened his shoulders and cracked his neck. A trickle of blood leaked from where the rifle butt hit his face. He smiled and then grimaced. He gingerly felt his jaw.

"You're all right, Tar. I don't care what everyone else says about you," Vig said. He gave us a thumbs-up and ran off the bridge.

"What a strange planet," Tar said.

I watched Vig's transport exit the ship and then

raised the ramp. I moved my hands over the control that started the engines. The ship rose off the ground and ascended into the air. The landing gear light went off and I activated the thrusters and began maneuvering the ship up into the atmosphere. Air traffic defense announced their disapproval on the speakers.

"Hirsute Razor, you're not authorized to leave this airspace. Please land at once."

I pressed the comm button and shrugged my shoulders.

"Uh, mission control, we are executing a standard ecto beast containment protocol, over."

There was a tense minute as we waited for the response. I looked at the defense systems for the ship and realized they were primarily for use outside a planetary atmosphere. It might get dicey if we had to fight before getting all the way out of their airspace.

"Roger that, Hirsute. Carry on and watch your abdomens. Mission control out."

"That won't always work," Tar said.

"It may never work again," I replied. I accessed the navigation systems and plotted a course for Tanjea. "Let's hope we can catch that ship before it reaches Tanjea."

"And before Barnabus is dead," Tar added and sat down. He poked a fork at the remains of the meal left there by the helmsman. He made a face. "Don't think I can eat while he's being eaten alive by an ecto beast."

"Baby ecto beasts."

"Oh, that makes it so much better."

CHAPTER 9
HOW MUCH IS THAT ECTO BEAST IN THE WINDOW?

We made it out of Progorian space with no pursuit in sight. I suspected thoughts of an ecto beast loose on board had dimmed the enthusiasm of any prospective pursuers. The Progorian cruiser performed admirably, closing the distance with the Tanjean transport quickly. We pushed the ship to its limits to catch our target as soon as possible, but it still took three hours to get there. We didn't know if Barnabus already floated inside an ecto beast or was still being prepared to serve as baby ecto beast formula.

Tar retrieved another laser rifle from the ship's armory. I picked mine up and checked the safety as our cruiser docked with our quarry. Our ship hung at a forty-five-degree angle connecting to the transport. Grappling magnets hung onto the other ship's hull, ensuring we wouldn't be parted until we finished our business. We went down to the docking port just in front of the crew quarters below. The green light went on next to it, the wheel spun and the hatch opened.

I looked through the short five-foot-long tunnel connecting the ships; I didn't see anything waiting on the other side. Tar took a deep breath and stepped into the tunnel first. I followed close behind, but not so quickly that I couldn't see an ecto beast rearing its head to skewer Tar. We emerged on the other side unscathed. Our noses wrinkled at the unfamiliar scent of an ecto beast ship. I thought it smelled like burning plastic and glue.

As I looked around, I saw different handholds and textures on the floor of the vessel, leading me to suspect this was a xeno-friendly transport not specifically designed only for ecto beasts or other Tanjean lifeforms, but ready to accommodate an inordinate number of races. Being a prisoner-consuming megastar on Progor Two must pay very well to afford such extravagance. We came to a small sealed room with a table in it. Barnabus lay unconscious on the table, a breathing mask on his face was attached to a long open-ended tube. His arms were bound to his sides and his legs strapped together. The cooking appliances and machines arrayed inside meant this room served as the galley. A large tube hung open at Barnabus' feet and attached to the wall.

"We gotta get in there," I said. Tar tried the door, but it was locked. He shot the lock. We pushed the door open manually and looked at the table.

Barnabus was gone.

"Huh," Tar said. We walked over to the table. The tube had a sign on it that read 'Bridge.'

"Simple enough," I said and we ran back out. A turbo lift at the end of the corridor had a green light next to it. We ran to the open door and got in. I pressed the button marked 'Bridge.' The door closed and the conveyance slowly moved upwards. Soft music started playing and the lighting dimmed.

"Doesn't really know what turbo means, does it?" Tar said. We looked at the controls, but there was nothing we could see to change the speed. Ecto beasts evidently didn't like to get anywhere too fast.

Several minutes later, we reached the bridge. As the door opened, we looked into a long corridor. I poked my head around carefully and didn't see anyone.

"Not a lot of crew on board," Tar said.

"I can think of a lot of reasons why an ecto beast would travel alone."

We cautiously walked by each room along the corridor, but they were all empty until we got to the bridge entrance at the very end. I opened the door and the ecto beast, a semi-transparent greenish glob with a head, arms and feet, looked at us. It stood under a tube like the one in the galley. We could see the outline of Barnabus floating inside the ecto beast. The long tube dangling from the beast's mouth looked very much like it could logically end in the mask we saw Barnabus wearing earlier.

"No proboscis to worry about," Tar said as we raised our rifles. The ecto beast raised its arms and they extended out fifteen feet at lightning speed, knocking the rifles out of our hands. The arms retracted and shot out at us again. I managed to drop and roll without getting hit. Tar wasn't so lucky and caught a tentacle across his forehead, ripping open the hastily stitched self-inflicted wound there. One of his subdermal horns lay on the floor of the corridor. Tar grabbed his head and screamed in pain.

I dove for my rifle and just avoided another hit from the ecto beast. Tar got struck full-on and sailed back down the corridor, sliding to a stop just a few feet from the turbo lift.

I came back up in a kneeling position and fired the rifle. It missed. The ecto beast hit my left arm with a glancing blow that probably would have broken the humerus if it had struck directly. As it was, I had a bleeding gash across my bicep. I raised the rifle with the other arm and fired. It blew the ecto beast's head off.

"Tar, you okay?" I shouted as I walked over to the ecto beast. The seared end of Barnabus' breathing tube stuck out from its neck, covered in light green slime. I flicked it with my finger and knocked most of the slime off it.

"I've seen better days," Tar said as he stumbled into the room, wincing. Blood streamed down the left side of his face and a bit of skin hung down above his left eye. I could see exposed skull on the left side of his forehead.

"If I was in perfect shape myself, I'd do this solo, but seeing as I'm having some problems with my left arm at the moment."

Tar pulled the knife from my left pocket, extended the blade to its full length and sliced down the center of the beast. The belly popped open and Barnabus tumbled out, still bound and covered with green slime. Several small neon green bulbs were attached to his body. The bulbs pulsed as they sucked the blood from Barnabus. They were still safe in the slimy cocoon around him.

Barnabus jerked awake and began writhing on the floor.

"This is bad," Tar said. I looked around the bridge

and saw a door leading off to what I hoped were the Captain's quarters. I ran in and found the shower. I set it to 'water' and turned it on. I came back out and grabbed one side of Barnabus with my right arm. By now, my left arm had gone numb. I figured there may be some poison in the ecto beast's tentacle that caused the numbness. I hoped it didn't travel throughout the body.

"Shower," I said. Tar grabbed Barnabus' other arm and we dragged him toward the shower. With our hands in the goo, we were fair game for the ecto beast's young which found us and latched in, beginning to suck the blood from both of us. We both screamed out in pain but we didn't drop Barnabus.

"I don't want to help babies get born today," Tar groaned as we reached the shower and shoved Barnabus in. As soon as the water hit, the slime deteriorated and, a few moments after being exposed to the air, the leeching ecto beast tadpoles dropped off, squirmed a few times and then stopped moving.

We rolled Barnabus over to get all the slime and babies off. I pulled the mask off his head and he screamed in terrible agony. We must've rinsed off a hundred offspring. Each one had latched into Barnabus' flesh. The wound where just one of them bit me burned like the wound was lined with acid.

Tar stabilized Barnabus with his foot and cut the binding straps off him using his uninjured hand. Barnabus just lay there, his body jerking as he screamed himself hoarse. I went back into the Captain's quarters and spotted an emergency medical kit on the wall. I pried it open with my ruined hands, tears in my eyes as I tried to read what was in the kit. I found a pain killer and stumbled back over to Barnabus, shoved the transdermal injector against his shoulder and pressed the button. Within a few seconds, he stopped screaming and curled up into a ball and shook.

I adjusted the dosage on the injector and gave myself a smaller dose. I popped one into Tar as well as he lay against the wall of the shower. Tar opened his eyes and looked at me.

"Good scavenging," he said. He looked at Barnabus, cold and shivering with nothing but water and open wounds to give him cover. "Let's get him out of here."

I turned off the water and we both grabbed Barnabus and dragged him out of the shower. I grabbed some blankets from the quarters' supply closet and covered him up on the floor. Even with the drugs, neither of us was in any shape to lift him off the floor onto a bed.

I heard a sound coming from the bridge.

"Aww crap, the ecto beast is regenerating."

CHAPTER 10
DON'T LET THE DOOR HIT YOU ON THE WAY OUT

We stumbled onto the bridge and saw the beast's half-open belly closing up. Part of its head had grown back. As the arms started to move and pulse, I picked up a laser rifle and shot at the rapidly developing brain stem. The ecto beast stopped moving.

"Where's the brig on this thing?" I said as I walked over to the ship controls. There was a selector on the compatibility screen that was set to 'Invertebroid.' I changed it to 'Humanoid.' Panels, switches and buttons emerged from the walls. I found a map of the ship and scrolled through the levels. The brig was on the same level as the kitchen.

Tar and I looked at each other. We looked at the large tube dangling over the ecto beast.

"Looks like we'll have to return our order to the kitchen," Tar said.

I located the program that controlled the kitchen delivery system and set it to reverse. The large green ball of ecto beast rose up into the air until it covered the opening. It disappeared rather quickly as the suction built up.

We got into the turbo lift and it moved down as fast as it normally would since we set the ship configuration to 'Humanoid.' I scratched my head for a moment. My hand came to rest on the stretched skin of the subdermal horn in my forehead.

"If ecto beasts don't like to travel fast," I said, "then the ride thru the tube was most likely unpleasant."

When the door opened, we stepped into the corridor and noticed a green light coming from the kitchen. We walked to the door and I observed a fine layer of green slime on the windows. We opened the door.

Every surface in the kitchen was covered in a mist of green slime and chunk of green, nearly transparent flesh. Small bits of translucent white cartilage protruded from some of the fleshy bits; I assumed this comprised the flexible skeleton of the ecto beast. Tar closed the door. "Don't think he's regenerating from that," Tar said.

"Glad we don't have to clean up the mess."

We returned to the bridge and walked toward the Captain's quarters.

"Get out," a voice said from near the command console. We turned to see Barnabus pointing a laser rifle at us. His long hair had sloughed off in chunks, probably from the ecto beast's internal juices.

"We came to save you," Tar said.

"From something you caused," Barnabus said. "If I'd never met you, none of this would've happened."

"We're sorry about that," Tar said. Barnabus fired the rifle at Tar, striking him in the left shoulder. The hit burned through the clothing and singed Tar's skin. "Aww come on!"

"That was the low setting," Barnabus said as he clicked the settings on the rifle. "Next one's a kill shot."

"Leaving," Tar said as he turned and walked to the door. I looked at Barnabus. The laser rifle was still on my shoulder. He set his lips in a straight line and I figured I might get a shot off, but it wasn't worth it. I put my hands up and grabbed the barrel tip with my fingers. I pulled the rifle off slowly and set it down.

"Barnabus," I said.

"I'll figure it out, Gorth. Whatever it is. Just leave."

I nodded and walked out to join Tar at the turbo lift. We got in and rode down to the kitchen level. As we passed the slime-encrusted kitchen, Tar smiled.

"He's going to be fine."

I looked at the kitchen windows. The slime still dripped.

"As long as he doesn't get hungry," I said.

We traversed the short distance back to our ship. I input the command on our side to disengage the port connection. The hatches sealed and the tunnel depressurized. The tunnel collapsed back into our ship and the cover slid shut over the apparatus. The three magnetic grapplers receded into their housings.

I watched the transport slowly float away from us and felt a calm wash over me. That was just a few seconds before the pain washed over me.

"Let's get to the medical bay," I said. Tar was already turned around and shuffling toward it.

"At least we're not dead," Tar said.

"For once. I agree with that sentiment."

CHAPTER 11
THE GREATEST DEATHS YOU COULD POSSIBLY EXAGGERATE

Over the course of the two weeks it took us to get back to Eleera, I managed to rig the medical machinery to remove our subdermal implants and restore our foreheads to their former shape and function without too much trouble. Most of our other injuries were easily handled, although the bites from the ecto beast offspring left a circular scar on our forearms and, anywhere the ecto beast slime had touched us, the hair grew back very fine if it grew back at all. I imagined Long Hair would no longer be known by that nickname.

Harquoth was surprising civil and friendly now that we had erased his smuggling charges and agreed to fence the Progorian cruiser for us at a mere fifty-percent cut. It was intergalactic highway robbery, but the amount of money we got from the sale was still substantial. That it was the infamous cruiser used by the intergalactic Claché criminal masterminds Tar

Reztap and Gorth helped the resale value immensely. Oddly enough, the buyer was a former Progorian Executional Administrator now elected Governor who preferred to remain anonymous. There was a note on the bill of sale to the former owners: 'Well done!'

When we returned to the Namreg, the inevitable communication request came in from Renni. Tar put it up on the screen in the bridge where we could both be equally amused and devastated by whatever Tar's half-brother had to say.

"Hey, big half-bro, what's happening?" Tar said as he kicked his feet up on the command console.

"Satisfied with yourselves, are you?"

Tar and I looked at each other and nodded.

"Yeah, I think so. We both came back alive," Tar said

"You killed thousands of people when you impacted a school, church and old folks home on Progor Two!"

"That's definitely a shame," I said.

"The first ceasefire in two centuries between the Progorians and Clachés is now a distant memory as they have increased their military production to full capacity! According to the news reports we intercepted, millions have already perished."

"Is that Progorian or Claché reports you intercepted?" I asked.

"Progorian, of course. The Claché are notoriously tight-lipped about war casualties. Monitoring their airwaves, you'd swear there wasn't even a war in progress much less the unbridled bloodshed that has transpired! What does it matter to you?"

"Doesn't," Tar said as he folded his arms. "Just curious."

"One thing I will say, your likenesses are all over the airwaves of both planets as Claché spies and the primary instigators of renewed intergalactic war. You're wanted for high treason by both races."

"Even the Claché government thinks we're Claché?" I asked. That seemed surprising.

"Your likenesses were transmitted in a fifteen-second war update and they carried the Progorian version of your faces, somewhat modified to appear more menacing, but they know your names nonetheless."

We looked at each other again and smiled.

"Yeah, I think we're all right with it," Tar said.

"This is a glaring example of my profound wisdom to never acknowledge our affiliation." Renni folded his arms and smiled. "I'm certain Mother will be proud of your accomplishments nonetheless, Reztap."

Tar inhaled sharply but said nothing.

"And," Renni continued, "to top it all off, you got poor Barnabus killed! Well, I suppose at least he won't be somehow implicated in your nefarious escapades with the Clachés and Progorians, may he rest in peace."

"May he rest in peace," we mumbled together. It wouldn't do Barnabus any good to be outed as being alive, so we both thought it better he remain officially—if not actually—dead. It was the Progorian way, after all.

The communication shut off. I felt a profound state of weariness wash over me. Tar shrugged his shoulders.

"That wasn't so bad—we're still alive!"

"About as successful as any other mission we've been on," I agreed and slunk off to my bunk for a long overdue nap.

PART TWO

DIGGING REZTAP

CHAPTER 1
A SIMPLE PLAN

It seemed like my family was always on the move. Given their expertise in the rare field of geological biology with a specialty in sentient minerals, they were in high demand across the Republic.

I spent months in the care of robotic babysitters on space stations while they excavated asteroids, atmosphere-less moons and planetoids, and the occasional lifeless planet ravaged by war or the natural violence of space. I once got to stay with a bored company engineer on a light science vessel rocketing through space as it kept pace with a dormant comet. The ball of ice and rock emitted what appeared to be intelligent radio waves in an undecipherable language. My parents descended to the comet's surface and discovered an ancient transmitter that had been part of a long-extinct species' war games. Not the scientific discovery they'd been hoping for, but it added to their notoriety and income just the same.

All of this traveling eventually brought us to the

mining colony on Nialus' fifth moon. It was there I met the most confounding and interesting person to ever wield a sonic jackhammer—Tar Reztap. My parents had no idea what they had germinated with this visit.

What brought my family to the colony in the first place was a local mineral scientist's discovery of a strange yellow crystalline structure growing in a rock substrate that shouldn't be there. The location of the discovery had been cordoned off years before, so the find was initially thought to be a brand new life form with a strange sodium chloride biochemical signature. After a three week investigation, however, they determined an errant construction contractor had vented his suit's urine tank somewhere he shouldn't have.

During that three weeks, I had the run of the mining colony with an annoying Mach Five, red and white sitter-bot, complete with extendable arms and creepy pink bug eyes, hovering over my every move. It was during a meal of grilled cheese sandwiches and gorglemelons under the impenetrable glare of the sitter-bot that I overheard a fair-skinned boy just a little smaller than me talking to a yucky girl.

"Grizelda, please reconsider. I've got two months of frundle harvesting and then I'm all yours," the small, curly-haired kid said. He actually got down on his knees and clasped his hands together. For a moment, I thought he was praying for forgiveness.

"Tar, if I'm not more important to you than some dumb farming contract, I have plenty of other suitors who think I am," the blonde girl in the shimmering silver sun dress said.

"What's a suitor?" I asked my sitter-bot. It blinked its big glowing pink eyes at me.

"Feer glog no," it responded. I sighed. I had disabled its speech subroutines and recognition so it couldn't tattle on me.

"You mean everything! But I'm under contract and-"

"Big words for a little boy. We're through!" the girl said and stormed off. Tar's shoulders slumped as he watched her go.

"Hey Tar," I shouted and waved my arms. Tar looked at me from where he knelt and frowned. He got up and walked over to me.

"Do I know you?" he asked as he sat down. He raised a hand and the table food kiosk delivered a nutritious meal on a tray to him.

"I'm Gorth."

"Um," Tar said and scratched his head. He stuck his fork in something purple and it ran off the table. "What planet are Gorths from?"

"I'm Terran. My name is Gorth."

"Gorth, huh? Sounds like a case of indigestion."

"And Tar is something they covered roofs with on Terra."

We stared at each other while we consumed our meals. Tar shrugged.

"Fair enough," he said. "So what brings you here? I hardly think a pampered-"

Before Tar could finish his insult, a high-pitched scream echoed throughout the cafeteria. We looked around and noticed the cavernous room had completely emptied while we finished our lunch.

Tar jumped up and ran to the entrance. I was right behind him with my sitter-bot puttering along in the air behind me. We entered the corridor that was hollowed out of the stone outside the cafeteria. We looked in both directions but there was no one in the corridor. I spotted some silver cloth on the ground.

"That looks like it came from Grizelda's dress," I said as I walked over to it.

Tar turned pale.

"No," he whispered.

Another scream came from somewhere. It echoed throughout the corridor, making it difficult to tell which direction it came from. My sitter-bot pointed to the left.

"Gershoff tok," it said.

"Come on!" I shouted and ran where the sitter-bot pointed. Tar was right behind me.

The corridor ended at a mining tunnel. Just in the distance, we saw a mining cart on the maglev tracks disappear around a corner. I spotted a small wisp of blonde hair drop into the interior of the cart.

"Well," I said as I turned to Tar. He wasn't there. Across the tracks, Tar was pushing another mining cart onto the tracks. He climbed in.

"You coming?" he asked. Sitter-bot put a yellow, metallic hand on my shoulder to hold me back. I smiled, pushed the hand away and climbed into the cart.

Tar pressed the acceleration control and the cart sped down the track. Brightly colored veins of different minerals blended together overhead as we gained on the other cart. Suddenly, in the cart ahead, a boy with spiky black hair poked his head up and laughed. Our cart swerved into another tunnel away from the other cart, which continued another direction. I saw a warning sign - this tunnel led to the smelter.

"We have to stop the cart!" I yelled.

"Brakes aren't working—hold on!" Tar said and pulled open the controller. He grabbed some wires and reconnected them, causing the cart to drop onto the tracks. A shower of sparks flew up around us as the cart spun in circles, slowed down and tipped off the tracks.

We tumbled over inside the mining cart. It came to rest on top of us—we were trapped but uninjured. A faint glow from the maglev tracks came in from one side, but was overwhelmed by the brilliant fiery light coming from the smelter on the other side. The interior of the cart lit up with an eerie orange glow.

"That was close," I said.

"It always is," Tar replied.

The sitter-bot lifted the cart off us.

"Joggle! Trif mon po! Squallatay!" it screeched.

"What's wrong with your bot?" Tar asked as he dusted himself off and looked at it curiously.

"I scrambled his vocal circuits so he couldn't report on me to my parents."

"Cool," Tar said. He looked at me and smiled. "You're not half-bad, Gorth."

I scratched my head.

"Thanks, I think."

Tar looked around. He pointed at a cart heading away from the smelter.

"Come on! That one just dumped its load and I think I know where Kelnick is heading," Tar said and ran after the cart.

I followed. Sitter-bot sighed as it dropped the upended cart. It puttered along and kept up with me. I'm certain its little circuits brimmed with annoyance. "Kelnick?" I asked as I climbed into the cart after Tar.

"The Merciless," Tar said as he manipulated the cart controls. "His dad is the magistrate here. He's a spoiled brat who thinks he can always get whatever he wants."

I nodded. During my travels, I'd dealt with many privileged kids. Some of them were okay, but I'd met my fair share of the worst childhood had to offer. Bullies set my teeth on edge.

Tar worked the controls expertly. His skill at piloting a mining cart were well beyond my own.

"How long have you been mining?"

We dropped down onto a lower maglev track.

"About six months," Tar answered.

"How old are you?"

Tar glanced back at me and shrugged. "I'm about your age—nine Androsian years are roughly the same as Terran years."

We rounded a tight turn and I grabbed the side of the cart for balance. The sitter-bot hovered in the air behind the cart, keeping pace with our crazed flight thru the mine.

"Don't you think that's a little young to be away from home?"

Tar shook his head.

"How old are you again?" he asked and we both ducked to avoid a dangling light fixture. A small clang echoed behind us as sitter-bot tangled with the light fixture. The bot and light fixture disappeared from view as we rounded another curve.

"Same as you, but my parents are here. Are yours?" We went down another tunnel for a minute and then started a steep climb.

"It's better here than at home. I'm the youngest of thirteen."

"I see. I'm an only child, but my mom is expecting another soon. I'll have a little sister."

We got to the top of the steep hill and I took in a deep breath. The cart teetered at the top of a long drop.

"It's not as dangerous as it looks," Tar said.

The sitter-bot arrived at my shoulder, looked at the incline and chittered wildly.

The cart started down the hill and we held on tight to the edges of the cart. The wind whipped thru Tar's curls as the walls of the tunnel began to blur. At the bottom of the drop, we plunged into darkness. I felt my stomach drop as we hit the curve in the track at the bottom and shot back up into the light.

"Treat your sister nice. The only real attention I get at home is from my half-brothers and sisters and it's all bad."

We came to an intersection. Tar licked his finger and held it up in the air.

"Wind's with us! We can beat them there," Tar said. I licked my own finger and held it up, but couldn't tell what he was checking. I suspected he was bluffing to impress me.

The cart rotated to the left and was off at a brisk pace again.

"What about your parents?" I asked. Sitter-bot appeared over my shoulder again, sporting several new dents. The little red M on its torso was missing some of its paint. It followed us a little unsteadily. I thought I detected a five-percent impairment in the left thruster.

"Mother's busy ruling the planet and Dad's building me a spaceship."

The cart stopped. I looked around and saw we were on a bridge. On the opposite end of the bridge, a dark tunnel spit out a cart driven by Kelnick. He hadn't noticed us and was coming in fast.

"Kelnick! Release her at once!" Tar yelled.

Kelnick looked at us and turned pale. He grabbed at his controls.

"Tar," I said. "I don't think he can stop fast enough."

"He's bluffing," Tar said.

We looked at Kelnick's cart. We looked at each other. Tar grabbed at the controls and we moved backwards.

It wasn't fast enough. The carts collided and our cart tumbled off the bridge. We screamed as we fell.

Sitter-bot grabbed our arms and pulled us back up to the bridge. Kelnick's cart teetered on the edge of the track, ready to fall off the bridge with the slightest nudge. We ran to it and pulled it back onto the tracks.

"Wow," Kelnick said as he stood up. "You do have it bad."

"I told you, Kelnick," Grizelda said as she stood up. "He has enough time to chase me, but not enough to keep me."

"This was all a ruse?" I asked.

Tar's mouth hung open as he looked desperately in his young mind for something to say.

Grizelda climbed out of the cart and walked up to Tar. She gently closed his mouth and kissed him. I grimaced at his misfortune.

"If you're man enough, Tar, I'll see you at the party," Grizelda said and walked back to the cart. "Come on, Kelnick."

Kelnick climbed out of the cart, sneered at us and then followed Grizelda. They walked off the bridge to a service turbo lift and disappeared behind the closing doors.

"Women," Tar said. He climbed into the cart and looked back at me. I jumped into the cart and it lurched forward.

PART THREE

ARMED BUT NOT READY

CHAPTER 1
EMPLOYEE SAFETY ISSUES

In our past meetings on Selatarn with our navigator headhunter, Tob, we typically met at Galloper's Interstellar Bar & Grille. As it so happened during this trip, our meeting had to be relocated due to Galloper's being temporarily closed while exterminators hunted down the crazed reptilian offspring of an expired patron. We never learned the exact race of the patron, but the offspring had killed four people already and they weren't taking any more chances. It was just bad for business.

Sigmund's Shady Emporium was a combination flea market, black market and soda fountain. As we walked in, half a dozen people walked by and then away from us shaking their hands. We had set bio-electric traps on our pockets to dissuade pickpockets.

"Ho!" Tob called to us from a booth near the front of the shop. We joined him in a well-lit booth, the seats being well sealed and verified by the Anti-Pickpocket League of Selatarn to allow no one to get through. Unfortunately, it hadn't been inspected in the nearly twenty years since the league had gone bankrupt and was now full of breaks and holes that any enterprising young thief could get his hands through. We still depended on our traps and carried the least amount of money we could get by on.

Tob stood up and greeted us, his wide gray beard flowing over his middle-aged paunch. His glowing red eyes sparkled as he greeted us. It was his gentle but rough looking, bark-like skin that really put a person at ease. The dryad-like Sonoffin were widely regarded as the most gentle of souls.

"Sorry for meeting you here like this," Tob said in his wispy voice. "But after the last three navigator deaths on your ship, the Navigator's Guild has been watching my office like a hawk beast. I've kept all credentialed navigators off my retainer list as a precaution, but just the other day I saw Silus Grenthal giving me the eye from across the avenue."

Silus was the man-at-arms for the Navigators' Guild. He didn't care for us the first time we laid eyes on each other years ago. With us reducing their paying membership every time a navigator died, he'd become even less friendly.

"Look, I explained all those to the guild. Mordu was a case of mistaken identity—we're not even sure that he's dead. Barnabus was an unfortunate victim of war, I told Vessix not to step in the acid pool, and Harneta...well, I'd never seen a particle deatomizer before so I had no way of knowing it would reduce her to atomic particles to be responsibly recycled."

"It was a recycling plant," Tob said.

"We were there to pick up a shipment. She just stood in the wrong place and I happened to lean on the right button."

"Hmm," Tob said.

"Wrong button. She also shed, so..." Tar shrugged his shoulders.

"And you explained all of this in excruciating detail to the Navigator's Guild Inquiry."

"Yes," Tar nodded.

"Even the shedding part?"

"I... I thought it was relevant at the time."

"And how did they respond?"

"Well, essentially they put me at the top of the list of the most dangerous captains in the galaxy and strenuously advised me to invest in an automated navigation system."

"In those exact words?" Tob looked intently at Tar, who kept his mouth shut.

"They said he was a menace and would never get another credentialed navigator again as long as the universe pulsed ions through matter," I said and tapped my fingers on the table.

"That's a long time," Tob said and nodded. Tar rolled his eyes.

"So," I said. "If you don't have any credentialed navigators..."

"Not to worry," Tob said with a smile. "I've arranged for a new navigator. He's not fully certified but is dependable and a hard worker."

"Why isn't he certified?" I asked.

"He had a tendency to crumble under pressure, specifically certification testing, but he knows his stuff and passed all his schooling at the top of his class."

"Well, thankfully our navigators are never put under any kind of pressure," I said.

"Beggars can't be choosers," Tar said. "Where is he now?"

"Well," Tob said, looking down at the table and sipping a bit of the Bropthorne Fizzie he'd ordered, "he got in a bit of trouble and is being held on bail in

Alagath on Herod Three. If you guys can bail him out, he's agreed to be your navigator."

"Why couldn't you bail him out?" Tar asked.

"Well, given the nature of his offense and history on the planet, they required bail to be paid in full and in person by a responsible party. I never leave Selatarn for too long. I'd lose my office lease."

"What was the nature of his crime?" I asked and sipped on my own Bropthorne's Fizzie. It was fruity and salty simultaneously.

"He urinated on the President of the planet."

"Urinated?" Tar asked.

"The Nynex are very jittery and he was so nervous when he saw the President at the guild hall, he lost control."

"He's a Nynex?" Tar stopped stirring his Bropthorne's Fizzie and stared at Tob.

"Sorry, didn't I mention that?"

Nynex are a few brain cells short of half a brain. They're a highly excitable primate humanoid with big yellow eyes. Arguments have gone on for years about whether or not they qualify as being a humanoid or an animal species. However, some of the most intelligent among them are easily passable for sentient.

"Has it really come to that?" Tar asked. He took his Brapthorne Fizzie and downed the whole thing. Tob's eyes got wide as he watched Tar twitch his nose for a few seconds. Tar opened up his mouth and let out a belch that rattled the windows. At the bar, a Nynex dressed in a loin cloth and a top hat jumped up on the bar top and rang a gong. Everyone in the shop cheered. The Nynex jumped back down behind the bar.

"It's really only for long hauls between systems," I said.

Tar sighed. "Alright. I suppose it's less expensive than a fully automated system."

"Well, not by much. Bail is three hundred thousand credits," Tob said and quickly sipped his own drink.

"Three? How many people did the guy pee on?" Tar asked.

"In addition to the President, the mayor, the governor's wife and two senators. But it was all at the same time."

"Oh, well, what a relief!" Tar said.

"And what a bladder," I added. They both looked at me. "What?"

Tar shook his head. "OK, provided he is fully clothed and wears a padded loincloth at all times," Tar said.

Tob nodded.

"He anticipated as much and agreed ahead of time if that was requested."

"Great, but what about Herod Three?" Tar asked.

Tob and I looked at each other in confusion.

"What about it?" Tob asked.

Tar looked at us and frowned.

"There's something making me uneasy about Herod Three. I just can't put my finger on it."

I shrugged my shoulders. I didn't recall anything bad about Herod Three.

"Their excise taxes are a little high, maybe?" Tob offered.

Tar folded his arms and stared at his empty glass. He shook his head.

"I got nothing but an uneasy feeling."

"Maybe you should wear a parka," Tob said. We both glared at Tob. "Or maybe not."

Chapter 2
Bargain Basement Navigator

Herod Three was a fully terraformed colony. Everything had been imported and life took root in various forms, shapes and sizes. Every species and variety was welcomed, resulting in a strange cross-breeding program that created new and unusual life forms.

After terraforming, Herod Three also supported a rich agricultural platform for many of the galaxy's strongest and healthiest crops. The citizens of Herod Three were almost ninety percent immigrants. An especially small hierarchy of colony founders and their families comprised nearly all of the highest forms of government on the planet.

Founded almost five hundred years ago, Herod Three started as a fifty-year terraforming project that evolved naturally ever since. Most considered the colony a must-see destination for rich tourists. Since

Tar and I had never considered ourselves rich tourists, Herod Three never made our list of must-see destinations. Tar's concern about coming here was as mysterious to me as it seemed to be to him.

Even after a two-week journey, the twenty-five-thousand-credit docking fee nearly had Tar turning the ship around. Only a careful explanation that this was our last chance to obtain a navigator for a long time caused him to relent and pay the fee.

As we rode down on the shuttle, we watched the lush forests rolling by, giving way to sun-washed marble terraces overflowing with greenery and sparkling waterfalls. The center of Herod Three's capital city, Alagath, was dotted with brilliant spires and ornamented geodesic domes that looked like they were made of diamonds.

"So this is how the rich live," Tar said.

"And the people who do menial jobs for them," I said. Tar grunted.

"It's a bit too pristine, don't you think?"

"Very," I said as the shuttle passed by a large, leather-winged creature that resembled a dragon floating lazily through the sky. "Amazing."

We landed at the star port and were welcomed with a basket of fruit and garlands of flowers. Tar waved his thanks and appreciation.

"I know we paid for it," Tar whispered to me. "But I would've rather had a discount and the bum's rush to the courthouse."

"Shame that wasn't an option," I said as I bit into a gorglemelon. I always wondered what it would taste like if it cost ten times as much. It tasted remarkably similar to the least expensive I'd consumed. I still finished it since I loved them with a passion.

As we stepped outside the star port, an automated

carriage made of transparent crystals and drawn by holographic stallions pulled up.

"Welcome visitors! Where would you like to go in the crystal city?"

"Good grief," Tar mumbled.

"Courthouse, please," I said before it could try to interpret Tar's remarks.

"Please climb on board. Watch your step."

The door on the carriage opened and a set of steps emerged from under the carriage to the ground. We stepped up into the carriage and sat down on transparent cushions that conformed to our bodies; it felt like we were melting into the nothingness of the carriage. As the doors shut, a holographic servant appeared between us. The carriage began to move and we floated casually through the city on a cloud of air and decadence.

"Would you like a beverage?" the holograph asked. I looked around and saw the city passing by through the completely transparent walls of the carriage. I couldn't even begin to guess from where this automated holograph would produce a beverage, but I was dying to find out.

"An Arwhalean ale, please," I said. The holograph nodded at me, paused for a moment, produced a frosted mug from within its jacket and proceeded to pump Arwhalean ale from its fingertip. When the frothy goodness reached the rim, the servant handed me the mug.

I admit it took a few moments before I closed my gaping jaw. I nodded to the servant and took a draught of the ale. The bitter hoppiness tickled my taste buds and the aroma dazzled my nose. The sharp tang of the Arwhalean blood fruit grabbed the back of my throat and danced a jig. It was a fine brew.

I toasted Tar. He rolled his eyes and looked out the window.

"An automated system would've been cheaper," I said.

"Almost, and it would've been less predictable. Even less than a Nynex with a penchant for freezing in the middle of combat."

"Think he'll freeze?"

"I think we'll lock him in a room with absorbent walls when we're about to go into combat."

"That's a good compromise," I said and took another drink. We stopped in front of a building that looked like it had been made of stars. The walls glowed with the fire of a thousand suns interspersed with the darkest blackness of empty space.

"We have reached your destination," the carriage announced.

"This is the courthouse?" Tar said. He shook his head. "No wonder it cost so much to bail someone out. They need the money to pay the light bill."

I finished my drink and we stepped out of the carriage. I turned to tip the carriage, but it sped out of sight before I could even turn around. Tar walked to the front door of the courthouse, shaking his head the entire time.

We entered the building and all the surfaces were comprised of the purest white marble we'd ever seen. At least it didn't glow. Tar walked up to the counter and a woman who could easily pass for a supermodel on any other planet smiled at Tar.

"How may I help you?" she asked. Tar just stood there with his mouth open. I sighed.

"We're here to pick up Harry Swizzelton," I said. The girl scrunched up her face, but still managed to look incredibly beautiful.

"The Nynex?"

"Yes, the Nynex," I said and smiled as big as I could.

"You know you could just pick one up at the corner pet store," she said.

"This one's a little smarter than your average Nynex," Tar said.

She raised her eyebrows and pursed her lips. She shook her head and punched a button on the counter anyway.

"Please prepare Harry Swizzelton for bail," she said.

"The Nynex?" came the response from the counter's speaker.

"That's what I said," she replied.

"Now I've heard everything. I can die a happy man."

The woman looked at us and smiled nervously. She looked at the computer system. Her eyes got wide. "You know you can just buy one for a thousand credits? Like two kilometers that way," she said and pointed to the right.

"We just really want Harry," Tar said.

"We have your payment on record. But you can just get a refund and leave..."

We shrugged simultaneously.

"It will be just a few minutes," she said and looked at her computer. She glanced around the room for a moment. "You know, I could come work for you for that much. I'm pretty handy with just about anything," she said.

"Do you know how to be a navigator?" Tar asked. She frowned.

"No, I'm just a licensed star ship pilot and lettered chef."

Tar and I looked at each other and then back at her.

"Why are you working here?" Tar asked.

"The benefits can't be topped."

"Well," Tar said. "We could use a chef."

"No, Tar, we need a navigator," I said. Tar frowned at me.

"Now I wish we'd gotten the automated system... and a chef."

A male cleared his voice to our left. We looked at a man who could've walked off a gym floor after pressing five hundred pounds and then ground granite with his teeth. In his left hand, he held the hand of a four-foot-tall primate dressed in an orange jumpsuit.

"This is Harry Swizzelton," the man said. I looked at the woman.

"Is that man a navigator by chance?"

"Physicist and literature scholar," she said, shaking beautiful blonde curls that flowed like water over her shoulders. I briefly considered giving in and getting a personal chef but put it out of my mind for reasons which I was certain I would punch myself for later.

"Of course, he is."

"Hey Harry, let's go!" Tar said. The Nynex responded by jumping up and down enthusiastically. He ran up to Tar and jumped in his arms, knocking Tar to the floor.

"You can keep the jumpsuit," the man said. "Maybe he won't pee on you." The man walked back into the offices behind the counter.

"Hi, Tar!" Harry said. "Sorry about knocking you down."

Tar picked himself up and nodded.

"That's okay. It's kind of how my day's been going.

Now let's get you out of here before anything else happens."

Tar walked out and Harry followed. I brought up the rear, but glanced back to see the beautiful woman at the counter raise her eyebrows in disbelief and shake her head again. In this instance, a chef looked a damn sight better than a navigator.

We stood at the edge of the sidewalk for a while. One or two empty carriages passed by, but none of them stopped even when we raised our hands.

"How peculiar," Tar said.

"They don't stop," Harry said.

"So I see," Tar said. "Thank you for stating the obvious."

"Don't stop for vagabonds."

"Wow, you're off to a great start with us, Harry."

"Vagabonds on Herod Three have net worth less than five million credits."

We both looked at Harry.

"They picked us up at the star port," I said.

"Courtesy ride for new tourists. Have to get credit check and pay ahead for more rides."

"Great, so how do we get back?" Tar looked around.

"Sidewalk," Harry said and pointed at a moving sidewalk so seamlessly camouflaged into the landscape we hadn't noticed it before.

"Ah, the preferred mode of transport for the riffraff," Tar said. We stepped onto the moving sidewalk. It brought us across the street to a central sidewalk directory. Harry pointed at the directory and we noted two sidewalk paths that eventually carried us to our destination.

"Look at him navigating already," I said. Tar gave me a dirty look and we walked toward the first sidewalk. We stepped on and moved toward our first connection.

"So Harry, how did you do in navigation school?" Tar asked.

"Ah, I climbed to the top of my class during each test."

"Great," Tar said.

"Umm, climbed?" I asked.

"Absolutely," Harry replied. He stopped and picked something out of the fur on his arm and ate it.

"You freeze during tests. How did you climb?"

"Girders on the ceiling. Got higher than anyone else in class," Harry said.

"So you didn't pass any tests," Tar said.

"I passed them all," Harry said.

"Really?" I asked.

"Yes, I passed on the tests by not taking them. I tried the first one, but I had an accident at the desk. After that, I climbed to the top of the class."

"That's it. We're taking you back," Tar said.

"No!" Harry said. "Tob said I could make your ship go zoom!"

"I bet he did," I said as we stepped off the moving sidewalk. Harry looked down at the ground. I looked around for another sidewalk going back the way we came. Tar looked around as well.

"Oh no," Tar said.

I looked in the same direction as Tar and saw an attractive redhead looking our way. An incredibly large animal with a bright red coat stood next to her on a leash; it looked like a mix between a lion and a bear.

"Who's that?"

"Anna Janus; we had a falling out. Now I remember why I didn't want to come here."

"Because?"

"She might want to kill me."

Anna dropped the leash and shouted "Sic 'em!"

The giant animal jumped in a ten-foot arc away from Anna and bounded down the sidewalk toward us.

Chapter 3
Cut Above the Rest

It's okay," Tar said. "That's an Algonquin Slicer Cat. Just stay perfectly still and it won't attack."

"Okay," I replied.

We looked down and noticed Harry had disappeared. We turned to see Harry running like mad across the various moving sidewalks, tripping and falling on each one as he got to them. The cat leaped over our heads in pursuit of Harry.

"Why does he have to be worth three hundred thousand credits?" Tar asked and ran after the cat. I kept up with Tar and we deftly navigated the sidewalks as we came to them. The cat neatly leaped over each sidewalk, never missing a step, gaining quickly on the Nynex. It almost caught up to Harry when the jittery primate darted into a building.

"Oh good, he found cover," I said before I saw the cat tear through the stone door like it was papier-mâché. We looked up through the transparent upper floors of the twenty-story-tall spire. Harry was traversing the stairs, heading for high ground. He made good time until about half way up when he slowed down and then stopped. He peeled his jump suit off and then continued on. The pause gave the cat the chance to gain on him.

We got to the building and ran to the elevator. It was open and ready for occupants.

I pressed the button for the 20th floor and the transparent cube rose into the air. We could see the frantic flight of Harry up the rest of the building to the roof. He closed the door and paused at it for a moment. I imagined he'd had the presence of mind to try to lock it.

We got to the top floor and ran to the door the cat had just finished tearing through. We got to within thirty feet of Harry and saw the Algonquin Slicer Cat slowly approaching its prey.

"Harry!" Tar shouted. "Stay perfectly still and it won't harm you."

Harry stood still as a bean pole. We breathed a sigh of relief until the cat paused and sniffed at Harry. A giant stream of urine pulsed from Harry's groin into the cat's face. It shook its face and growled.

Harry panicked and ran to the edge of the roof. The cat sliced off Harry's left arm and leg with its claws, grabbed him in his mouth and shook him. It flung Harry up in the air. He landed at our feet. His severed arm and leg dangled precariously on the edge of the roof.

The cat turned toward us and advanced slowly.

"Fluffy, no!" Anna said. She had taken another elevator and just arrived. The cat stepped back to the edge and sat down.

"Harry," Tar said as he knelt down. He tore strips off his shirt and tied tourniquets around the arm and leg stubs. "It's okay. We can get your arm and leg reattached."

The cat purred and its tail lazily wagged behind it, knocking the severed arm and leg off the roof. They fell unimpeded to the sidewalk twenty stories below.

"Maybe not," I said. Tar looked back at the cat and saw the now empty roof edge.

"We'll figure something out," Tar said.

Harry screamed out in pain.

"Sorry about your pet. At least they're only a thousand credits. Guess that makes us even," Anna said. She clicked her tongue. The Algonquin Slicer Cat walked to her and they left the roof.

"Three hundred thousand, actually," Tar said as he held Harry's hand.

The courthouse only gave Tar a partial refund of his three-hundred-thousand-credit bail, since he could only return seventy-five percent of the prisoner for trial. Tar spent the greater bulk of the refunded credits on artificial limbs and other medical bills for Harry who semi-retired to a quiet life on a tropical island where he served drinks to crazy rich tourists who liked having a cyborg Nynex waiter.

As we left Herod Three two-hundred-and-fifty-thousand-credits poorer, I looked at Tar and smiled.

"At least we're not dead," I said. He turned his back on me and wouldn't talk to me for a week.

THE REZTAP CHRONICLES

BOOK ONE: THE ADVENTURES OF REZTAP

Even simple plans never quite work out for intergalactic trader Tar Reztap, and yet he and his loyal friend Gorth keep finding their way into crazy missions that border the impossible. Chased throughout known space aboard the Bloated Namreg (quite possibly the ugliest ship to ever dock in a space port), it's not long before Reztap's nemesis catches up. And it's not the captain of the Progorian warship (really, it was an honest mix-up that started the war); nor the Madame of the Courtesan Academy, who happens to be a half-sister to the head of the assasin's guild. No, real trouble requires blood ties. Reztap's half-brother sends the traders spinning back into space on a mission to rescue a princess from a fortress on Alaga One's moon.

Desperate times call for desperate measures, and Reztap and Gorth are forced to pull out their back-up navigator—an eccentric android named Chuck, who has a thing for decorating (and "Rezzy"). Aboard the Namreg, a door that couldn't be opened for thirteen years mysteriously grants entrance to a hidden chamber. Inside is a treasure, a long-lost family member, and a mission no one has to force Reztap to do. But this time, he can't fail. Regretfully, the "rescued" Princess Slurk is still on board, with plans of her own.

BOOK TWO: THE QUEST FOR THE INSANE MOTH

As they acclimate to the newly revised ship and crew, Tar and Gorth try to retrieve the scarf lost in the battle with The Insane Moth. Against his mother's demands, Tar drags everyone to the remote and extremely hostile planet of Rimtiki Lumdung. Things seem to be going well as they infiltrate the populace until their plans are thwarted by an old flame of Gorth's—the beautiful and extremely deadly Zeestra.

To escape with their lives, the crew must fight against an ever shortening time line to remove an ancient curse that has plagued the planet for centuries. Will Tar and Gorth live through the ordeal while fighting zombies dead, alive and otherwise? Or will Zeestra's treachery seal their fate and end their adventures forever?

www.ingramcontent.com/pod-product-compliance
Lightning Source LLC
Chambersburg PA
CBHW060559100726
47907CB00005B/1432